Have You Seen My New Blue Socks?

by Eve Bunting

Illustrated by Sergio Ruzzier

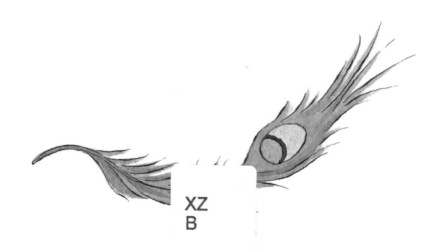

Clarion Books | Houghton Mifflin Harcourt

Boston | New York | 2013

Clarion Books
215 Park Avenue South,
New York, New York 10003

Text copyright © 2013 by Edward D. Bunting
and Anne E. Bunting Family Trust
Illustrations copyright © 2013 by Sergio Ruzzier

Clarion Books is an imprint of Houghton Mifflin Harcourt Publishing Company.
www.hmhbooks.com

The text was set in Pastonchi MT Std.
The illustrations were done in pen & ink and watercolor on Arches paper.

LIBRARY OF CONGRESS CATALOGING-IN-PUBLICATION DATA

Bunting, Eve, 1928–
Have you seen my new blue socks? / by Eve Bunting ;
illustrated by Sergio Ruzzier.
p. cm.
Summary: The reader is invited to help Duck
and his animal friends find a missing item.
ISBN 978-0-547-75267-9 (hardcover)
[1. Stories in rhyme. 2. Lost and found possessions—Fiction.
3. Socks—Fiction. 4. Ducks—Fiction. 5. Animals—Fiction.]
I. Ruzzier, Sergio, ill. II. Title.
PZ8.3.B92Hav 2013
[E]—dc23
2012012192

Manufactured in China
SCP 10 9 8 7 6 5 4 3 2
4500400904

To Marlene and John Bunting with love
—E.B.

To Giev, Nava, and Pearl
—S.R.

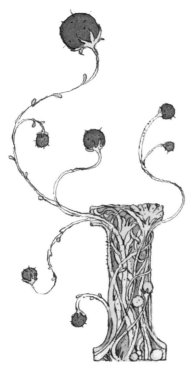 have

lost

my new

blue

socks.

Did I put them in my box?

I know I put them somewhere near.
How could they simply disappear?

I will ask my friend the fox.
"Have you seen my new blue socks?"

"I have not seen your new blue socks.
Did you look inside your box?
Did you ask your friend the ox?"

"I will ask him right away.
I will ask this very day."

"I have lost my new blue socks.
Have you seen them, Mr. Ox?"

"Did you look inside your box?
Did you ask your friend the fox?
I may have seen your new blue socks—
I saw some socks down on the rocks."

"Thank you, thank you, Mr. Ox!
I'm off to find my new blue socks."

These are socks, but they're not new.
They're more like purple, not like blue.

I'm trying not to be depressed.
Without my socks I feel undressed.

I'll ask the peacocks—they might know.
They're always strutting to and fro.

"Peacocks? Have you seen my socks?
I did not put them in my box.
I asked my good friend Mr. Fox.
I asked my good friend Mr. Ox.
Peacocks? Have you seen my socks?
They are such a pretty blue!
I just got them. They are new."

"Are those you're wearing now the same?"

"The same? Oh, no!
That can't be right!
All my other socks are white."

"But I can see a touch of blue
underneath your laced-up shoe!"

"I'm *wearing* them? I put them on?
I was certain they were gone.
I knew I put them somewhere near.
I did not know I put them here!"

"Thank you, thank you, dear Peacocks.

At last I've found my new blue socks!"